Zoë
at Fairy School

for Duncan and Oliver

Designed by Louise Millar
Printed and bound in Belgium by Proost
for the publishers Piccadilly Press Ltd.,
5 Castle Road, London NW1 8PR

ISBN: 1 85340 635 X (hardback)
1 85340 640 6 (paperback)

3 5 7 9 10 8 6 4

A catalogue record of this book
is available from the British Library

Jane Andrews has two sons and lives in Slough in Berkshire.
Since graduating from art college she has undertaken a variety
of graphic work, including illustrations for magazines.
This is her first children's picture book.

Zoë
at Fairy School

Jane Andrews

Piccadilly Press • London

It was Zoë's first day at Fairy School.
She was so excited that she couldn't sit still.
"How can I straighten your wings
if you keep buzzing about?" laughed her mother.
"You'll never fly properly if I don't!"

Zoë's best friend, Pip, was waiting for her
at the end of their street.
"Hurry up!" called Pip, as Zoë flew into view.
"We can't be late for our first day!"

When Zoë and Pip arrived at Fairy School
the elves and fairies were chattering and giggling,
twirling and tumbling all over the place.
One naughty elf gave Zoë a pinch!
Then suddenly everyone went quiet . . .

. . . as the beautiful Fairy Queen appeared
in a flash of light and sparkles.
"Welcome everyone!" she said. "I am your head teacher.
This is my assistant, Ms Tooth Fairy. And this is
Mr Mischief, who will be teaching the elves."

"Now, everyone, find a toadstool to sit on – fairies here,
and elves over here," said the Fairy Queen.
Everyone rushed to the nearest toadstool.
The Fairy Queen turned to the fairies.
"Our first lesson is – how to wave your magic wand!"

All the fairies watched as the Fairy Queen
waved her wand in an elegant swoop.
The air was filled with a shower of scarlet sparkles.
"Oh dear," said Zoë as she tried to make her wand move
in exactly the same way as the Fairy Queen's.
"I don't think I'll ever be able to do this."

Pip could do it after just three goes, but Zoë
couldn't get her hand to swish up, down and across.
The wand kept pulling her up and up, or down and down.

Suddenly she gave a jump. A naughty elf had crept up
behind her and was pulling her wings.
And he was laughing at her!

Zoë felt like crying and she closed her eyes
to blink the tears away.

When she opened them, the prettiest butterfly she had
ever seen was fluttering near the end of her wand.
She watched the butterfly zip from flower to flower –
in a lovely, elegant arc.

"Swoop!" cried Zoë, and followed the butterfly's flight with her wand. The air crackled.

"Swoop!" cried Zoë again, starting to enjoy herself.

Her arm moved in a graceful wave and suddenly a bright shower of glittering sparks burst from her wand.

"Bravo, Zoë!" exclaimed the Fairy Queen.

"Your wand work is excellent. Look girls, see how Zoë does it. It is perfect. You must follow her example!"

Zoë couldn't believe her ears. The first day at
Fairy School and she had earned a gold star!

Zoë was so enjoying waving her wand that she didn't even care when the naughty elf stuck out his tongue at her. She concentrated hard, waved her wand – and turned him into a toad!

Zoë and Pip were very tired when they flew home that evening. But they both agreed that Fairy School was more fun than anything they'd ever done before!